Owlkids Books

DINOSAUR
DANCE-OFF

WRITTEN BY
Jorden Foss

ILLUSTRATED BY
Sara Theuerkauf

Darwin the dinosaur loved to dance.

He grooved
and he moved
in his skinny jean pants.

He swayed to music
no one had heard—

a cool indie band
led by Suet the Bird.

Darwin skipped, and he spun,

and he flew through the air.

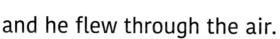

He tumbled, he rumbled,

and bumped with fresh flair.

Dancing is great
but more fun in a group,
so Darwin yelled out,

"Someone, join my troupe!"

He searched
high and low,

he looked
far and wide.

Who could Floss
to his level?

One, Two
Step?

Cha Cha
Slide?

Darwin giggled at that.
"Mom and Dad can't dance!
Their bones are too brittle—
they don't stand a chance."

His parents smiled at each other
and bound in without care.

Their moves were straight-up Jurassic,
and, to Darwin, seemed rare.

The Sprinkler,

the Shovel,

their Lawn Mower
was prime.

The Running Man
turned it up,

and . . . **Stop!** Darwin time.

Darwin's mom
said to him,

"There's no
time for a
break.

Come '**Jump! Jump!**' with me—

let's make this house shake!"

Darwin laughed and he laughed,
then his jaw hit the floor
when Grandma twirled in
with a big dino-ROAR!

She danced 'round the room
and said, "Those moves are fine,
but this fossil's got grooves
that get better with time."

She did the Twist
with a shout:

"These
moves
aren't
extinct
yet!"

From Cabbage Patch
to Harlem Shake,
the troupe's moves were fly.

The Jive, Waltz,

Pop and Lock . . .

They gave the Hitchhike a try.

The song finally ended
with a loud cymbal

smash,

and the group hit the ground
with a prehistoric

crash.

His dad smiled and said,
"Now that's dancing old-school."
Darwin realized then . . .
his folks were *actually* cool.

Exhausted from dancing,
Darwin crawled into bed.

His mom Moonwalked in
with a kiss for his head.

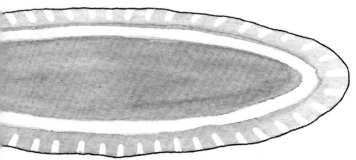

She said, "Sleep tight, little Darwin.
Tomorrow's a big day.

We'll teach you the Macarena

and the YMCA."

So Darwin fell asleep
and dreamt of his crew,
Mom, Dad, and Grandma,
and all their fresh moves.

For my little dancing dinosaurs,
Jude and Lennox —*J.F.*

With love and gratitude to my family and
friends for all their encouragement —*S.T.*

Text © 2022 Jorden Foss | Illustrations © 2022 Sara Theuerkauf

Owlkids Books acknowledges the financial support of the Canada Council for the Arts, the Ontario Arts Council, the Government of Canada through the Canada Book Fund (CBF) and the Government of Ontario through the Ontario Creates Book Initiative for our publishing activities.

Published in Canada by Owlkids Books Inc., 1 Eglinton Avenue East, Toronto, ON M4P 3A1

Published in the US by Owlkids Books Inc., 1700 Fourth Street, Berkeley, CA 94710

Library of Congress Control Number: 2021939044

Library and Archives Canada Cataloguing in Publication

Title: Dinosaur dance-off / written by Jorden Foss ; illustrated by Sara Theuerkauf.
Names: Foss, Jorden, author. | Theuerkauf, Sara, illustrator.
Identifiers: Canadiana 20210218460 | ISBN 9781771474412 (hardcover)
Classification: LCC PS8611.O7863 D56 2022 | DDC jC813/.6—dc23

The artwork was created in watercolor and pencil with digital enhancements.

Edited by Ella Russell | Designed by Alisa Baldwin

Manufactured in Shenzhen, Guangdong, China, September 2021, by C & C Offset
Job #HV4090

A   B   C   D   E   F

ONTARIO ARTS COUNCIL
CONSEIL DES ARTS DE L'ONTARIO
an Ontario government agency
un organisme du gouvernement de l'Ontario

Canada Council   Conseil des Arts
for the Arts   du Canada

Canadä

Publisher of Chirp, Chickadee and OWL | Owlkids Books is a division of   bayard canada
www.owlkidsbooks.com